TO

FROM

DATE

# Mommy's Favorite SMELL

Brock Eastman **and** Elsie Mae Eastman | Illustrated by David Miles

HARVEST HOUSE PUBLISHERS
EUGENE, OREGON

Cover design by Mary Eakin Design

Interior design by Left Coast Design

HARVEST KIDS is a trademark of The Hawkins Children's LLC. Harvest House Publishers, Inc., is the exclusive licensee of the trademark HARVEST KIDS.

## Mommy's Favorite Smell

Copyright © 2019 by Brock Eastman
Artwork © 2019 by David Miles
Published by Harvest House Publishers
Eugene, Oregon 97408
www.harvesthousepublishers.com
ISBN 978-0-7369-7476-9 (hardcover)

Library of Congress Cataloging-in-Publication Data

Names: Eastman, Brock, 1983- author. | Eastman, Elsie, author. | Miles, David, 1973- illustrator.
Title: Mommy's favorite smell / Brock and Elsie Eastman ; illustrated by David Miles.
Description: Eugene, Oregon : Harvest House Publishers, [2019] | Summary: Illustrations and easy-to-read text follow Little Lion and Mommy Lion through their day, as Little Lion anxiously tries to find her mother's favorite smell.
Identifiers: LCCN 2018061374 (print) | LCCN 2019000552 (ebook) | ISBN 9780736974776 (ebook)
     ISBN 9780736974769 (hardcover)
Subjects: | CYAC: Mothers and daughters—Fiction. | Odors—Fiction. | Love—Fiction. | Lions—Fiction. | Christian life—Fiction.
Classification: LCC PZ7.E126774 (ebook) | LCC PZ7.E126774 Mom 2019 (print) | DDC [E]—dc23
LC record available at https://lccn.loc.gov/2018061374

**Printed in China**

19 20 21 22 23 24 25 26 27 / LP / 10 9 8 7 6 5 4 3 2 1

**Brock**

To my wife for inspiring this amazing idea.

**Elsie**

To my Mommy, Kinney, Wavey, Deckie Boy, and Daddy, because I love you all.

**David**

To my wife wonderful wife, Carrie (who smells amazing!). Thank you for supporting me and this crazy career of mine. I love you!

Little Lion sniffed the air as Mommy Lion took a pan of delicious-smelling cinnamon rolls from the oven. Mommy Lion frosted one and set the gooey treat on Little Lion's plate.

Little Lion licked her lips and breathed in the aroma. This was her favorite smell. Was it Mommy's too?

"Mommy, Mommy, is this your favorite smell?"

Mommy shook her head. "It's sweet indeed, but the yummy scent of cinnamon rolls is not my favorite."

"What is it then? Oh Mommy, Mommy, will you please tell?"

"Little Lion, keep sniffing to find my favorite smell."

Little Lion followed Mommy Lion into the nursery. Baby Lion's diaper was stinky and needed changing.

Little Lion pinched her nose with one paw and fanned the air with the other. "Mommy, Mommy, is this your favorite smell?"

Mommy Lion shook her head and held the diaper out. "The smell of dirty diapers is not my favorite!"

"Oh Mommy, Mommy, will you please tell?"

"Little Lion, keep sniffing to find my favorite smell."

Mommy Lion smiled after taking a long sip from her morning latte.

Little Lion smelled vanilla and coffee—two flavors her parents loved. "Mommy, Mommy, is this your favorite smell?"

Mommy set down her steaming mug. "This coffee is smooth and delicious, but this aroma is not my favorite."

"Oh Mommy, Mommy, will you please tell?"

"Little Lion, keep sniffing to find my favorite smell."

Little Lion and Mommy Lion swung on the porch swing while a spring shower watered the flowers. The scent of grass and dirt filled the air.

Little Lion grinned. "Mommy, Mommy, does the rain make your favorite smell?"

Mommy Lion held a paw into the rain. "The smell of rain is sweet, but it is not my favorite."

"Oh Mommy, Mommy, will you please tell?"

"Little Lion, keep sniffing to find my favorite smell."

Little Lion was muddy and wet from playing in the yard after the rain. Mommy helped take off her dirty clothes and put them in the washing machine. Mommy had once said she enjoyed the smell of warm, clean laundry.

"Mommy, Mommy, is that your favorite smell?"

Mommy Lion held up a soggy shirt. "This will smell good when it's clean, but that's not my favorite."

"Oh Mommy, Mommy, will you please tell?"

"Little Lion, keep sniffing to find my favorite smell."

Daddy Lion brought Mommy Lion a bouquet of tulips.
She gave Daddy Lion a hug and kiss.

This *had* to be Mommy Lion's
favorite smell. She looked so happy.
"Mommy, Mommy, is this your
favorite smell?"

Mommy Lion put the bouquet in
a vase on the table. "Tulips
are my favorite flower, but
this fragrance is not
my favorite."

"Oh Mommy, Mommy,
will you please tell?"

"Little Lion, keep sniffing
to find my favorite smell."

Little Lion watched Mommy Lion take a batch of chocolate chip cookies out of the oven. She had used her great-great-great-grandma's recipe, and the aroma filled the whole kitchen.

Little Lion gasped—the chocolate chip cookies smelled so good! This had to be it. "Mommy, Mommy, is this your favorite smell?"

"This is a favorite treat. But my favorite smell isn't something that I eat."

"Oh Mommy, Mommy, will you please tell?"

"Little Lion, keep sniffing to find my favorite smell."

Little Lion followed Mommy Lion to the compost pile. Mommy Lion used the compost to fertilize her prize roses.

Little Lion pinched her nose as she dumped her bucket into the heap. This smell wasn't what she expected Mommy Lion to like, but still she asked, "Mommy, Mommy, is this your favorite smell?"

"My favorite smell? No, certainly not."

"Oh Mommy, Mommy, will you please tell?"

"Little Lion, keep sniffing to find my favorite smell."

Little Lion spent the rest of the afternoon sniffing everything she could find.

Was it the smell of the orange that Mommy Lion peeled?

It wasn't the smell of the rotten Easter egg she found outside.

And apparently the old-car smell of the minivan was not as nice as the new-car smell it once had.

Again and again Little Lion asked, "Mommy, Mommy, is this your favorite smell?"

And again and again, Mommy Lion replied, "This is not my favorite smell."

"Oh Mommy, Mommy, will you please tell?"

"Little Lion, keep sniffing to find my favorite smell."

The Lion family sat around their fire pit, roasting marshmallows. This was one of their favorite things to do together. Little Lion sniffed the air.

"Mommy, Mommy, do you love the smell of a campfire?"

Mommy Lion looked closely at her marshmallow.
"Campfires make great memories, but the smell
is not my favorite."

"Oh Mommy, Mommy, will you please tell?"

"Little Lion, keep sniffing to find my favorite smell."

The day was almost over, and Little Lion had
not found Mommy Lion's favorite smell.

She smiled, and her pointy teeth sparkled.
Then she blew. "Mommy, Mommy,
is this your favorite smell?"

"Your breath is minty fresh, but toothpaste
isn't my favorite smell," Mommy Lion said.

"Oh Mommy, Mommy, will you please tell?"

"Little Lion, keep sniffing to find
my favorite smell."

Little Lion had not found Mommy Lion's favorite smell,
and since it was time for bed, her search had to come to an end.

Little Lion nuzzled into Mommy Lion's side and asked one
last time, "What's your favorite smell?"

Mommy took a long sniff of Little Lion's fur and then
smelled Baby Lion too. "You, my little one," Mommy
Lion said. "There is no smell I love more than you."

"Me?" Little Lion asked.

Mommy Lion pulled her closer. "Yes, you."

"Even when I smell bad?" Little Lion asked.

Mommy Lion grinned. "That only means
it's time for a bubble bath."

Mommy Lion leaned over and
touched her nose to Little Lion's.
"Your smell reminds me of the first
time I held you and the first time
I said, 'I love you.'"

Little Lion sniffed the air.
"And your smell reminds
me of hugs and kisses.
Of feeling safe and
knowing I'm home.
I love you, Mommy."

We are to God the pleasing aroma of Christ among those who are being saved and those who are perishing.

*2 Corinthians 2:15*

**Prayer**

Jesus, thank You for giving me my nose and my ability to smell. Thank You for a world full of smells. I love You, Jesus. Amen.

**Questions to Ask Your Child**

What is your favorite smell?

What smell do you not like?

# An Activity to Do with Your Child

## Ashley's Amazing Chocolate Chip Cookies

### Ingredients

2¼ cups all-purpose flour

1 T. baking soda

1 cup butter, softened

¾ cup packed brown sugar

¼ cup white sugar

1 (3.4 ounce) package instant vanilla pudding mix

2 eggs

1 tsp. vanilla extract

2 cups semisweet chocolate chips

### Directions

1. Preheat oven to 350 degrees.
2. Sift together the flour and baking soda; set aside.
3. In a large bowl, cream together the butter, brown sugar, and white sugar.
4. Beat in the instant pudding mix until blended.
5. Stir in the eggs and vanilla.
6. Blend in the flour mixture.
7. Stir in the chocolate chips and nuts.
8. Drop cookies by rounded spoonfuls onto ungreased cookie sheets.
9. Bake for 10 to 12 minutes in the preheated oven. Edges should be golden brown.

**Brock Eastman** is the author of the Quest for Truth series, the Imagination Station series Showdown with the Shepherd, the Hippopolis series, and *Daddy's Favorite Sound*. He writes for *Clubhouse* and *Clubhouse Jr.* magazines and often speaks to schools and writing groups. Brock currently works for Compassion International, whose mission is to release kids from poverty worldwide. **www.brockeastman.com**

**Elsie Eastman** is seven years old and loves to dream, dance, and draw. Baking with her mommy is one of her favorite hobbies. She also enjoys sitting in her daddy's office, inspiring him by creating new characters and artwork. This is her first book, and she hopes to illustrate her own book or one of daddy's someday. **www.elsieeastman.com**

**David Miles** has been blessed to illustrate for many amazing publishers. He has worked on numerous children's books, book covers, magazine articles, puzzles, games, and more Bible stories than he can keep track of! David is currently working full-time as an illustrator and is probably drawing right now! You can see more of his work at **www.davidmiles.us.**

Join Little Lion and her family for more fun in
*Daddy's Favorite Sound.*